A Sheepdog Called Sky

Jasmine scooped the little dog up in her arms and held it close. The puppy opened its amber eyes and looked at her, and the tip of its tail slowly began to wag. The look in its eyes was one of absolute trust.

Also by

HELEN PETERS

LOOK OUT FOR:

A Piglet Called Truffle

A Duckling Called Button

A Kitten Called Holly

FOR OLDER READERS:

The Secret Hen House Theatre

The Farm Beneath the Water

Evie's Ghost

A Sheepdog Called Sky

HELEN PETERS

illustrated by
ELLIE SNOWDON

nosy
crow

First published in the UK in 2017 by Nosy Crow Ltd
The Crow's Nest, Baden Place, Crosby Row
London, SE1 1YW, UK

Nosy Crow and associated logos are trademarks and/or registered
trademarks of Nosy Crow Ltd

1 3 5 7 9 10 8 6 4 2

A CIP catalogue record for this book will be available from the British Library.

Printed and bound in the UK by Clays Ltd, St. Ives Plc

Papers used by Nosy Crow are made from wood grown in
sustainable forests.

ISBN: 978 0 85763 911 0

www.nosycrow.com

For my sister Hazel
H. P.

For Sarah and Daisy
E. S.

Chapter One
A Tiny Whimper

Jasmine and her best friend Tom were shovelling pig feed into a bucket when Jasmine suddenly remembered something.

"Guess what?" she said. "I'm going to be looking after two chinchillas in August."

Tom's eyes lit up. "Oh, chinchillas are so cute! Whose are they?"

Jasmine picked up the bucket. "They belong to one of the other vets at Mum's surgery," she said, as they crossed the farmyard towards the orchard. "They're called Clover and Daisy. They've got this massive cage and it's going to go in my bedroom. I can't wait."

A large mallard drake waddled across the yard towards them, flapping his wings and quacking. Jasmine laughed as he nibbled at her wellington boots.

"Don't be jealous, Button," she said, stroking his silky feathers. "You know you're the best duck in all the world. And Clover and Daisy are only coming for two weeks. You're mine forever."

Tom and Jasmine had rescued Button in the spring, when he was just an orphaned egg on the riverbank. Jasmine had given him his name because his perfectly round eyes looked like two shiny black buttons. He was a fully grown drake now, living happily with the chickens, but he still liked to follow her around the farmyard and be petted.

"Are you getting paid to look after the chinchillas?" asked Tom.

"I don't know. If I do, I'll need to give the money to Dad, for Truffle's feed. She eats so much these days. But that's the whole point of having animals to board, isn't it — so that we have enough money to look after rescued animals."

The two friends were planning to set up an animal rescue centre and boarding kennels when they grew up. The idea had been inspired by Truffle, Jasmine's pet pig, who was now trotting across the orchard to greet them. She had been a tiny runt piglet on the point of death when Jasmine had smuggled her home from a neighbouring farm and nursed her back to health eight months ago.

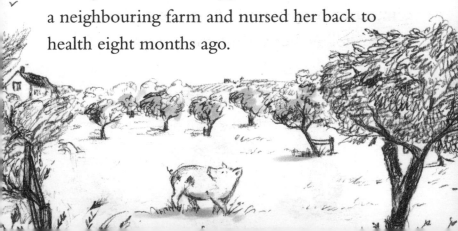

Tom tipped the feed into Truffle's trough and Jasmine scratched her behind the ears as she gobbled the pignuts.

"When are the chinchillas coming?" asked Tom.

"Not until the middle of August. Three weeks to go."

When Tom had to go home for lunch, Jasmine walked up the farm track with him. Fluffy white clouds perched high in the bright blue sky.

"The sky looks like a painting, doesn't it?" said Jasmine.

"It's better than a painting," said Tom, "because it changes all the time."

"Like a new painting every day."

In the field to the left of the track, Jasmine spotted her five-year-old brother Manu and his best friend Ben, crouched by a clump of hawthorn bushes.

"Look what we found!" called Manu.

"Ugh," said Tom. "That's creepy."

 4

It was an animal's skull, with big eye sockets and a complete set of teeth.

"Look, it still works," said Ben. He moved the lower jaw to make the mouth open and shut.

"It's a badger," said Manu. "We've got a leg bone, too. We're looking for the rest of it."

"I'm hungry," said Ben.

"There's biscuits at home," said Manu, and they ambled back towards the house.

Jasmine said goodbye to Tom at the end of the track. As she turned to walk back home, a little sound made her stop. Frowning in concentration, she stood still and listened.

The air hummed with insects. Bees buzzed in the clover and butterflies fluttered among the dog roses and rosebay willowherb. In the next field, a kestrel hovered, waiting to pounce on its prey.

I must have imagined it, she thought. She started to walk on. But then she heard it

5

again. A tiny whimper. It seemed to be coming from the hedge.

Jasmine walked back and scanned the thick hedgerow. There was no sign of an animal. She dropped to her knees and looked underneath the hedge.

And then she saw something. A heap of matted black and white fur. Was it a dead animal? A badger, perhaps?

The heap of fur whimpered again. Jasmine moved closer so she could see it properly.

A dog! A little collie, hardly more than a puppy, by the looks of it. But it wasn't a normal, healthy puppy. It looked barely alive. Its eyes were closed and its bones jutted out beneath the dull, matted fur.

"Hello," said Jasmine softly. "Hello, little dog. What are you doing under there?"

The puppy whimpered again, but it didn't move.

"Are you hurt?" Jasmine asked. "Are you

6

stuck? Let me get you out of there."

She reached in and gently put her arms around the little dog. She picked it up and gasped in shock. It was much lighter than she had expected. Its hip and shoulder bones stuck out from its body, and she could see every one of its ribs under the matted coat.

"Oh, my goodness," she said. "Oh, you poor, poor thing, you're starving."

The puppy lay limp in Jasmine's arms, taking

fast, shallow breaths. She tried to stand it up but it just flopped down again on its side in the grass. It clearly had no strength at all in its legs. It didn't even seem to be able to lift its head up.

Jasmine looked at her watch. Her mum, who was a vet, would still be taking morning surgery at the practice where she worked, four miles away. Jasmine could phone her and ask her to bring medicines and supplies, but she wouldn't be able to get back for at least an hour. Dad had gone to collect some new beef calves from a neighbouring farm. Jasmine's older sister, Ella, was at home, but she wouldn't have a clue what to do with a sick puppy.

Jasmine scooped the little dog up in her arms and held it close. The puppy opened its amber eyes and looked at her, and the tip of its tail slowly began to wag. The look in its eyes was one of absolute trust.

Jasmine bent down and kissed the top of its head.

 8

"Don't worry, little dog," she said. "I'm going to take you home and make you better. You'll be all right now. I promise."

Chapter Two

What Have You Brought Home Now?

Jasmine's heart was beating very fast as she walked home, cradling the dog in her arms. After that one sign of life, the puppy had closed its eyes again and had made no further movement. Jasmine had seen enough sick animals to know that, despite her reassurances, the little dog was very close to death.

The farmhouse was silent as she opened the front door and walked into the hall. There was an empty biscuit tin on the kitchen table. Manu and Ben must have eaten all the biscuits and gone out again.

Cradling the silent, unmoving puppy, Jasmine fetched a pile of clean towels from the airing cupboard and put them on the kitchen table. Then she carefully laid the dog on the towels on his side.

It was a horrifying sight. The little dog, whom she now saw was a boy, was barely more than a skeleton covered with a thin layer of skin and tangled, dirty fur. There were bare patches and sores on his skin where the fur had rubbed off in places, and he also had sores under his tail.

Jasmine took a deep breath. You need to calm down and think like a vet, she told herself. You've spent enough time watching Mum at work. What would Mum do now?

If the dog was starving, he was probably also very dehydrated. Gently, she pinched the skin on his neck, as she had seen Mum do. Instead of springing back when she let go, like normal healthy skin would, it stayed puckered up. The dog was extremely dehydrated. She needed to get some liquid into him.

She found a clean dog bowl in the scullery, filled it with water and carried it carefully to the table. She set it beside the dog, but he didn't move. Gently, she lifted his head and slid the bowl under his mouth, still supporting his head. To her delight, he opened his eyes, put out his tongue and started to lap the water.

"Good boy!" said Jasmine. "Good boy, you're drinking!"

She held his head until he stopped lapping, and then gently laid it down again. Stroking his ear, she considered him thoughtfully. "If you can drink," she said, "then maybe you could manage to eat something, too."

Mum had special canned food for sick dogs at the surgery, but until she came home, the best thing to tempt the puppy would be chopped cooked chicken.

Jasmine opened the fridge. Dad often made himself a chicken sandwich for lunch. Sure enough, there was half a cooked chicken breast left in an open pack on the middle shelf. Jasmine took it out. Dad would have to have a cheese sandwich today.

Taking a chopping board from the dresser, she cut the chicken into tiny cubes and put them on a saucer. "I don't know if you'll be able to eat," she said to him, "but let's see."

She lifted his head and slid the saucer under his mouth. To her amazement, the little dog

wolfed down the entire lot, licking the saucer
clean afterwards. Jasmine smiled at him as she
laid his head back down.

"Well done, little one," she said, ruffling his
tangled fur. "You're doing really well."

She walked over to the dresser, picked up
the phone and dialled the number of the vet's
surgery where her mum worked.

"Leconfield Veterinary Practice," said the
woman on the other end. Jasmine recognised the
voice of Mina, one of the nurses.

"Hello, Mina," she said. "It's Jasmine. Could
you give a message to my mum, please?"

"Your mum's right here," said Mina. "She's just finished with her last client. I'll hand you over."

"Hello, Jas," said Mum. "Is everything OK?"

"When you come home," said Jasmine, getting straight to the point, "could you bring a drip and a drip stand, please? And some of that special canned food for sick puppies."

There was a slight pause at the other end of the line. Then came a heavy sigh. "Oh, Jasmine," said Mum. "What have you brought home now?"

Chapter Three
I Can't Let
Him Down

Half an hour later, the front door opened.
Jasmine hurried into the hall to meet her
mother. Mum looked tense as she carried a
tall drip stand and a big case full of equipment
and medicines into the kitchen, but as soon as
she saw the little dog lying on the table, her
expression changed to one of horrified concern.

"I found him under the hedge by the lane at
the top of Hawthorn Field," said Jasmine. "He's a
boy. I checked."

"You poor little thing," said Mum, stroking the

dog's tangled coat. "What happened to you?"

"He weighs hardly anything," said Jasmine, "and he can't even stand up."

Mum went over to the sink and washed her hands. "Let's move him into the scullery," she said, "and examine him properly. You can be my nurse, Jasmine. You can start by wiping down the scullery surfaces. Where are the boys?"

"I don't know," said Jasmine, as she took a clean cloth from the cupboard under the sink. "They ate all the biscuits and went out again."

"Good," said Mum. "Hopefully they won't want lunch for a while, then. Dad can make them sandwiches when he gets back."

Mum brought the puppy on his heap of towels through to the scullery, and laid him on the work surface. His eyes were closed and he made no attempt to move.

"He's really dehydrated," said Jasmine. "I pinched his skin and it didn't spring back."

"Have you tried giving him anything to

drink?" Mum asked.

"Yes, I gave him a bit of water. He can't lift his head on his own but he drank when I held his head up. And he's eaten, too."

Mum shot Jasmine a worried look. "What did you give him?"

"Some of that cooked chicken breast, chopped up really small."

"Not too much?"

"No, just half a breast."

"Good girl. We mustn't overfeed him. Little and often is the key. Same with water."

"That must be a good sign, though, isn't it," said Jasmine, "if he's eating and drinking?"

Mum looked at the dog and then at Jasmine.

"I'm afraid this is a very sick dog, Jas."

Jasmine was so scared to ask the question that she could hardly breathe, but she had to know the answer.

"Will he survive?" she asked.

Mum paused. "To be honest," she said eventually, "I don't think he has much of a chance. The problem is, his internal organs will have been put under so much pressure from the starvation that he could suffer from organ failure at any time. We'll do our best, of course. But you have to understand, Jasmine, that a dog this emaciated is unlikely to survive and, even if he does, he might have lasting damage to his organs."

"You should have seen the look he gave me

 19

when I told him I was bringing him home," said Jasmine. "And he wagged his tail. He trusts me, Mum. He trusts me to make him better. I can't let him down."

Mum stroked Jasmine's hair. "We'll do our very best. Now, let's give him a thorough examination. Go and fetch the bathroom scales, and get a pen and paper, too. You can make a chart to record the results."

When Jasmine returned with the scales, Mum lifted the puppy on to them.

"4.2 kilos," she said. She laid the dog back on the towels. "Write that down, Jas. You'll need to divide your paper into columns. Put the date in the first column. Then you need columns for weight, temperature, pulse, treatment, drugs and feeding. You can fill the details in every day."

While Mum got the equipment ready, Jasmine divided the sheet of paper into seven columns and wrote a heading at the top of each. She filled in the date and then, under "Weight", she wrote

 20

"4.2 kilos".

"How much should he weigh?" she asked.

"I'll examine his teeth in a bit," said Mum, "to get a better idea of his age, but if he's what I reckon, which is about five months old, then he should weigh three times that. He weighs less than a cat, poor little thing. Now, wash your hands and then you can help me with the drip."

Jasmine had seen Mum setting up a drip before, but this was the first time she had been the head nurse. She held the little dog and talked softly to him as Mum shaved the hair from his right foreleg and cleaned the area with antiseptic. She held the catheter in place while Mum taped it to the dog's leg and attached the fluid line.

"Since he's drinking," said Mum, "he should only need to be on the drip for a few hours. It will just help to rehydrate him and get some nutrients into him."

"I won't leave you," Jasmine said to the puppy, stroking his head. "I'll stay with you the whole time."

"Now we need to give him a thorough examination," said Mum. "You can fill everything in on the chart."

First, Mum took the puppy's temperature to check for hypothermia, and then she checked him all over for bleeding and any obvious broken bones. "He seems to be all in one piece," she said, "so I don't think we'll need to X-ray him. You can dress these sores once I've examined him."

"How could anyone starve and abandon a puppy like this?" said Jasmine.

"It's hard to imagine, isn't it," said Mum. "When he's well enough to go to the surgery, I'll scan him for a microchip. If he's microchipped, we can trace the owner."

"You won't give him back, will you?"

"Well, that will depend. He might have run away, of course. But it looks more like a case of neglect and abandonment. We'll report the owner to the RSPCA, and they'll investigate."

 22

"I hope they put the owner in prison for a very long time," said Jasmine.

She stood by the little dog, stroking him and talking to him, breaking off only to add notes to her chart, as Mum checked his eyes and ears for infections and gave his paws a thorough inspection. The dog lay on his side, with his eyes shut, not moving an inch. Mum listened to his heart through her stethoscope and then gently palpated his tummy. Finally, she parted his lips to look at his teeth.

He stayed completely still.

"I think he's about five months' old," Mum said. "Poor little thing. You haven't had much of a life, have you?"

She unwrapped a new syringe from its sterile packaging. "I'm going to get a blood sample and take it to the surgery. It will tell us if there's any damage to his liver and kidneys."

She gave Jasmine a serious look. "Try not to get too attached to him, Jas. If he's not responding to treatment in a couple of days, I'm afraid it might be the kindest thing to put him down."

"That won't happen," said Jasmine, "because he'll be much better by then."

Mum sighed. "Well, let's hope so. It's lucky you found him when you did. He might not have survived another day in this state. He'll need a multivitamin and iron jab to give him a boost, and an antibiotic to prevent infection, and then I'll clip his coat around the sores and clean them out. You can get a bed ready for him. Use that plastic dog bed in the shed and line it with newspaper and Vetbed. I'll buy some nappies while I'm out, too."

"Baby's nappies?"

"Yes, we use them on dogs sometimes, if they can't move."

Jasmine fetched the plastic dog bed from the shed and wiped it clean. Then she lined it with old newspapers and Vetbed, an absorbent, padded material that vets used for sick animals' beds because it was easy to wash and dry.

"Once he's off the drip, you can give him a bath, and then he can sleep in here for now," said Mum. "You'll need to turn him regularly, to avoid putting pressure on the sores. Now, I'd better go and see what havoc those boys are causing."

Left alone with the puppy, Jasmine stroked the back of his head.

"You've had a horrible time, haven't you," she

 25

said, "but from now on, everything's going to be different. I don't know what your name was before, or if you even had a name, but I'm going to call you Sky. I'm going to look after you all the time and you're going to get better."

The little dog opened his beautiful amber eyes and looked into Jasmine's. And, very slowly, the tip of his tail began to wag.

Chapter Four

Don't Look At Me
Like That

Nine days later, Manu and Ben were making cupcakes at the kitchen table when Jasmine came in to find a snack. Ben was beating the eggs vigorously into the butter, scattering droplets of mixture all around the kitchen. Manu was weighing the flour, clouds of white dust flying into the air as he tipped it from the bag into the scale pan.

"What would you rather have?" Manu was saying. "Eyes that, when you blink for more than a second, they take a photo of what you were

27

looking at and the photo comes out of your mouth, or ears that, when you press them, they play any music you like, or teeth that, when you tap them with your fingers, you can play a tune, like on a piano?"

Ben sneezed into the mixing bowl. "Photo eyes," he said, wiping his nose with the back of his hand. Jasmine made a mental note not to eat any of the cupcakes.

"Me too," said Manu. "Is it eight ounces or eighteen ounces, Ella?"

Jasmine and Manu's sixteen-year-old sister, Ella, was officially in charge of their baking. She was sitting at the other side of the kitchen, hunched over a pad of paper she had balanced on one knee. A large book was balanced on her other knee. She was scribbling notes on to the paper, completely absorbed in the holiday research project she had been set as preparation for her A-Level English course. Manu had to repeat his question twice before she realised someone was speaking to her.

"Eight," she said. "All the ingredients should weigh eight ounces."

"Oh," said Manu. "I thought that looked a lot." He started scooping spoonfuls of flour back into the bag, sending more white clouds into the air.

Jasmine took two bags of crisps from the snack cupboard and went back to the scullery, closing the door behind her. Tom was kneeling on the floor next to the dog bed, stroking Sky's head. "Good boy, Sky," he was saying. "You're such a good boy, aren't you?"

Sky looked up and wagged his tail. He could move his head without help now, although he couldn't yet support himself on his legs. He was eating five or six times a day, but he was still very thin. It would be a while before he reached a normal body weight.

Jasmine took a box of dog biscuits from the cupboard above the work surface and Tom gently lifted Sky into a sitting position. Sky couldn't do this by himself yet, but he could stay sitting up on his own once he was in position.

Jasmine held out a biscuit in the palm of her hand, slightly away from Sky's mouth. Sky stretched out his neck to gobble it up.

"Good boy," said Jasmine softly. "Good

stretching. Well done. Let's see if you can stretch even further."

She laid another biscuit on the floor, slightly further away this time. Again, Sky stretched out his neck, shot out his pink tongue and gobbled up the biscuit.

"Good boy," said Jasmine. "You're getting stronger, aren't you?"

"Let's put him in his harness for a bit," said Tom.

Jasmine had made the harness to help Sky

regain the use of his legs, after Mum had told her about similar contraptions. Sky's harness was a wide strip of towelling sewn into a loop and attached at the top to a piece of rope that hung from a hook Dad had fixed to the ceiling. Jasmine put Sky in it for short periods each day, to help him support himself and build up his muscles.

Tom scooped Sky out of his basket and held him upright while Jasmine slipped the harness over his head and front legs. She smoothed out the fabric so that it stretched under his belly from his front legs to his back legs. Then Tom took his hands away, so that Sky was in a standing position with his legs on the floor.

"I think he's putting some weight on his front legs," Jasmine said excitedly, after Sky had been in the harness for a while. "Look, they're not just dangling any more, are they? Clever boy, Sky. You're getting stronger."

At the sound of her praise, Sky looked

adoringly at Jasmine and wagged his tail.

"He's so cute," said Tom. "Do you think you'll be allowed to keep him?"

Jasmine looked at Tom incredulously. It had never even crossed her mind that she wouldn't be allowed to keep Sky. "Of course I'm going to keep him," she said.

"You're so lucky," said Tom. "I wish I could have a dog."

"You can help look after Sky any time you like," said Jasmine.

Through the clattering and chattering in the kitchen, Jasmine heard Mum's car pull up outside.

"I want Mum to see Sky standing in his harness," she said, opening the door from the scullery into the kitchen just as Mum opened the other door that led into the kitchen from the hall. Her partner at the vet's surgery, David, was behind her.

Mum's eyebrows shot up and her mouth

dropped open. Ben and Manu fell silent as they registered the shock on her face. They looked sheepishly at the table, the floor, the dresser top and then at each other. Every surface, including their faces, was covered in dustings of flour, sprinklings of sugar, smears of butter and trails of egg white. Broken egg yolk oozed across the floor, and there was a pattern of footprints where they had trodden in egg and flour and walked it across the tiles.

"Where's Ella?" asked Mum.

The boys looked around vaguely. "I don't
know," said Manu. "She was here."

Mum took a deep breath. "Well, go and find
her, and ask her to come and help you clear
up this mess, right now. And take your shoes
off before you go upstairs," she said, as the boys
headed for the door.

"Yes, Nadia," said Ben, as he shuffled past her.
"Thank you, Nadia. Sorry, Nadia."

Ben was always extremely polite to adults.
It meant that he got away with all kinds of
outrageous behaviour.

"Sorry about that," Mum said to David. "Just
my son and his friend in typical style."

David gave a polite smile. He didn't have
children. And after visiting their house, Jasmine
thought, he probably wouldn't want any.

"David's come to give a second opinion on a
cow, so he popped in to see how Sky's getting
on," Mum said to Jasmine.

"Your mum says you've done a great job with

him," said David. "He was
such a sad little thing when I
saw him last week."

"Come and look," said Jasmine.
David had last seen Sky the
day after she had found him,
when Mum had taken him
into the surgery to give him
his injections and a scan. She
hoped he would see a real
difference now.

Sky was still in his harness. Tom was kneeling
on the floor beside him, stroking his back. Sky
looked up and wagged his tail as Jasmine came
in.

David's eyes widened. "Wow," he said. "That's
remarkable. I wouldn't have recognised him."

At the sound of David's voice, Sky's tail tucked
between his legs and he shrank back, baring his
teeth in a low growl.

"It's all right, Sky," said Jasmine, sinking to her

knees beside the skinny little dog. "David's a vet. He won't hurt you."

She looked up at David. "He's like this every time he hears a man's voice," she said. "He's the same with Dad. We think a man must have been cruel to him."

"Poor little thing," said David softly. "The RSPCA haven't traced anyone yet?"

"No, but they're still trying," said Mum. The scan had revealed that Sky had not been microchipped, so Mum had reported the case to the RSPCA as well as the local dog warden.

Sky was relaxing slightly now, as Jasmine stroked him and murmured comforting words in his ear.

"He looks so much healthier," said David, still speaking softly so as not to frighten Sky, "and his coat's much better already."

"Jasmine's bathed him and dressed his sores every day," said Mum. "And he's eating and drinking well now."

"He's starting to support his weight, too," said Jasmine. "Look, Mum, he's using his front paws."

"You're doing a wonderful job with him," said David. "I'm really impressed."

"I'll give the rehoming centre a call," said Mum. "At this rate, he'll be ready to go there in a few weeks, if nobody claims him."

Jasmine froze. Then she stared at Mum in horror. "What are you talking about? Sky's not going to a rehoming centre."

"He has to go eventually, Jasmine," said Mum. "Oh, don't look at me like that. You surely didn't think you were going to be able to keep him for ever?"

Chapter Five
I Have to Keep Him Now

Jasmine stared at her mother in outrage. "Of course I'm going to keep him," she said. "He loves me and I love him. He's already been abandoned by one owner. He's not going to be abandoned by another one."

"Jasmine, a dog is a huge amount of work," said Mum. "It won't be like Truffle or Button, where they grow up very quickly and can just live on the farm. Sky will need hours of attention every day for the whole of his life, and that might be fourteen years or more."

"I know that," said Jasmine. "I've read all about looking after collies."

"Then you'll know how much work they are. How are you going to manage that when you're at school all day?"

"Only from nine till three. And I bet Dad would like to have him around while I'm at school. I'm going to train him as a sheepdog when he's old enough, so he'll be a help to Dad."

David was looking increasingly uncomfortable. "I'd better go and look at this cow," he said. "Where is she?"

"She's in the old bull pen," said Mum. "Michael should be around. He's probably feeding the calves. Thanks, David. And sorry about the chaos."

"Are you still going to be all right to look after the chinchillas," David asked Jasmine, "or will you be too busy with Sky?"

"Oh, no, I'll definitely look after the chinchillas," said Jasmine. "It's school holidays now, so I've got plenty of time."

As soon as David had left the room, Jasmine said, "I can't believe you're thinking of sending Sky to the rehoming centre! Do you want him to spend his life in a cage, looking out through the wire with sad hopeful eyes, like all those other poor dogs? How can you even bear to think of it?"

Jasmine's parents had taken her to visit the rehoming centre once, and had vowed never to do so again after she had begged to take home every animal in the place.

Sky started to whine.

"See?" said Jasmine. "He knows. You've upset him."

"He's upset because he can tell you're upset," said Mum.

"So don't upset me, then."

Mum raised her eyebrows warningly. "I don't think we should be having this conversation in front of Sky," she said. "Or Tom, for that matter.

 41

Sorry, Tom."

Jasmine followed her into the kitchen, which looked marginally less chaotic than before. Ella was sitting in the corner reading her book. Manu and Ben were at the table, stirring a vast quantity of blood-coloured liquid in Mum's largest mixing bowl.

"What on earth is that?" said Mum.

"Icing," said Manu. "For the cupcakes."

"But that's far too runny. And why have you made such a ridiculous amount?"

"It was a bit stiff, so we added more water," said Ben, glancing at Manu. "But my elbow got jogged and I think we might have added a bit too much."

"So then we put in all the rest of the icing sugar," said Manu. "Two whole bags of it, but the icing's still runny."

"Sorry, Nadia," said Ben.

Mum gave Ella an exasperated glance. "Ella, you promised you'd supervise them."

42

A Sheepdog Called Sky

 43

"I did," protested Ella, "but if you take your eyes off them for even one second, they do things no normal human being would ever think of. Like pouring in the entire bottle of red colouring and filling the whole bowl with water."

Mum gave a heavy sigh. "Leave that icing, boys, and go and do something else. Something quiet and clean. I'll sort the icing out later."

"Let's go and put that cow's tooth we found in our collection," said Manu. He looked around the table. "Where is it?"

"In one of your pockets, probably," said Mum. "That's where I usually find things, right before they go in the washing machine. If I'm lucky, that is."

Last month, the washing machine had broken, and when the repair man had been called out, at great expense, he had found several small bones and teeth inside it.

"It's not in my pocket," said Manu. "Oh, now

I remember, I took it out of my pocket and put it on the table, right there, before we started making the cakes."

Everyone looked at the table. There was no sign of a cow's tooth. Everyone turned their gaze towards the Aga oven where the cupcakes were now cooking.

Ben grinned. "It will be a lucky dip," he said. "And the prize will be a lucky cow's tooth."

Jasmine sighed impatiently. "Anyway," she said to her mother, "Sky's attached to me now, so it would be cruel to give him away."

Mum turned her attention to Jasmine. "Firstly, Jas, we still don't know what happened to him. His owner might come and claim him. So there's no point even discussing it yet."

"But his owner was cruel to him! You can't let him go back."

"We don't know that for certain. Legally, we have to wait a month before rehoming him, to give an owner time to come forward. And if he does need to be rehomed, I'm sure there are plenty of people who would love a beautiful dog like Sky. It wouldn't be safe to have him here, with his fear of loud noises. It wouldn't be fair to expect Manu to be quiet all the time."

"It would be perfect," said Ella, "but sadly not possible in this world."

Manu looked hurt. "I can be quiet," he said. "And I want to keep Sky. Ben and me are going to train him to search out animal bones."

"You are not," said Jasmine. "I'm going to train him properly. I've already been reading about it. And Dad wants a sheepdog."

"His fear of men's voices could be a real problem, too," said Mum. "There are always people visiting the farm and walking through on the footpaths, and we can't have him lashing out and biting. We'd get in terrible trouble."

"He doesn't bite!" said Jasmine indignantly.

"He hasn't done so far," said Mum, "but we don't know what he might do if he was really frightened. And what about the cats? They might not appreciate having a collie around the place."

"Jasmine!" called Tom, from the scullery. "Come and see this."

Jasmine dashed in. Sky was standing in his harness. He fixed his amber eyes on her adoringly and wagged his feathery tail.

"He's putting his weight on all four legs now, I'm sure he is," said Tom.

Jasmine crouched down and felt his legs. He certainly seemed to be supporting his own weight.

"Let's take him out of the harness," she said. "Come on, Sky, we'll see if you can stand up by yourself."

She lifted the puppy up and Tom slipped the harness back over his head and front paws. Holding her breath, Jasmine gently set him down on the floor. He stood there, on his own four paws, gazing lovingly at Jasmine and swishing his tail.

Tom and Jasmine grinned at each other. "Oh, Sky," said Jasmine. "You are the best dog in all the world."

Mum opened the door from the kitchen.

"Look!" said Jasmine.

"Oh," said Mum softly. "That's amazing. I didn't think he'd even survive, and now he's standing up by himself."

"So," said Jasmine, "I have to keep him now, don't I?"

But Mum still wore the serious expression that meant she wasn't yet convinced. "I know he's gorgeous, Jas, and you've given him fantastic care and attention. I do know how attached you are to him, honestly. And you'll have him for a few more weeks, until he's fit enough to go to the rehoming centre."

Jasmine opened her mouth to protest, but Mum carried on. "All those things I said before still apply," she said. "It's a huge commitment, taking on another dog, especially a collie, and I just can't make that commitment at the moment."

Chapter Six
Shut the Cage
Door Carefully

Despite what Mum had said, Jasmine did not give up hope. She was certain that no owner would come forward, and her plan was to turn Sky into such a model dog over the next few weeks that the whole family would want to keep him.

The question of the cats, at least, was easily resolved. Toffee and Marmite had taken no notice of Sky at all while he was a helpless little invalid, but the first time he walked towards them on his own four feet, they crouched low to

the ground and hissed so ferociously that poor
Sky slunk out of the room with his tail between
his legs.

"Angela says that means the cats have
established their dominance over him," Jasmine
told Tom two weeks later, as she clipped Sky's
lead to his collar and they walked down the
garden path.

Angela was Tom's aunty, and she had
been helping Jasmine to teach Sky the basic
commands of collie training. She owned a collie
called Jake, whom Jasmine had looked after in
the May half term while Angela was away.

"Now she says the rest of us have to establish
our dominance over him, too," said Jasmine.

"That sounds mean," said Tom.

"It's not mean, it's just because dogs are pack
animals," said Jasmine, "so they need to know
who's pack leader. And they have to be bottom
of the family pack, otherwise they won't behave.
We have to show him we're always kind and fun

to be with, but also that we're always in charge, and that we have all the best toys."

In the garden, they let Sky off the lead. This was as much freedom as he had been allowed so far. He still wasn't fully protected by his injections, and also he wasn't fit enough to go for long walks yet. But the big garden was a perfect place for training sessions.

Sky began to sniff about happily in the long grass. As soon as he had moved a few metres away, Jasmine called his name. He looked up

enquiringly, his ears pricked. She called him
again and he trotted over to her.

"Good boy!" said Jasmine, dropping to her
knees and ruffling his fur. "Good dog!"

"He's learning really well, isn't he?" said Tom.

"He's good like this, with just us and nothing
to distract him, but I think it will be a while
before we can let him off the lead in the yard."

A flapping of wings made them both turn
round, just in time to see Button flying over
the low hedge and landing on the lawn. The

 53

moment Sky saw Button, he sank to the ground, his ears flattened back and his eyes fixed on the duck.

"Down!" commanded Jasmine, sweeping her arm down at the same time, palm downwards. "Good boy, Sky! Good boy!" she said, crouching beside him and ruffling his coat.

"But he was already down," Tom pointed out.

"That's how you train them to understand the command. If you say it every time they begin to go down, then eventually they learn that's what they must do when you say it at other times."

She moved a few paces back from Sky. "Stay!" she commanded, her arm outstretched with the palm outwards.

Sky's eyes remained fixed on Button. He began to slink towards the duck. Jasmine stepped between them.

"Stay!" she commanded again.

Sky continued to slink forwards. Jasmine repeated the command, trying to stay calm

 54

and preparing to grab Sky if he pounced. To her great relief, Button flapped back over the hedge. Sky got up and trotted over to sniff in the flowerbed.

"Hmm," said Tom. "That one might take a while."

"That was a bit scary," said Jasmine. "It definitely wouldn't be safe to take him out on the farm yet. Not with all the chickens around."

"Let's see if he can play a finding game, like Truffle used to," suggested Tom.

"Oh, yes," said Jasmine. "If I go and hide behind a tree, he'll probably follow me anyway, so while I'm going off and hiding, you say, "Find Jasmine!" all the time, and then when he gets to me, I'll praise him. If we do that a few times, he should get the hang of what he's meant to do."

Sky followed Jasmine everywhere like a shadow, so he naturally followed her when she went to hide. Once they had done it several times, with Tom calling out the command repeatedly and Jasmine praising him extravagantly when he reached her, Tom decided to keep Sky on the lead while Jasmine hid. When Tom let him off the lead and said, "Find Jasmine!" Sky ran to her instantly.

"Good boy!" said Jasmine. Sky rolled on to his back and Jasmine tickled his tummy while he wriggled to and fro, wagging his tail in delight.

Mum came down the garden path. "David's here with the chinchillas," she said. "Can you two help him bring their cage in?"

Jasmine, Tom and Sky ran up the path. In the farmyard, David was sliding a large wire cage out of his car. It was a big car and he had put the back seats down flat, but the cage still filled the entire space.

He looked up as they came out of the garden gate. "Hello, you two. Can you take one end of this? If it's too heavy, I'll take the branch out."

The cage had a big tree branch inside it, stretching from the solid wooden floor right to the top. Lots of smaller branches grew out from the big one.

"Where are the chinchillas?" asked Tom.

"They're in a carrying case on the front seat. We'll get the cage in place and then we can put them in it."

They took Sky to the scullery and then helped David carry the cage upstairs. It took up most of the free space in Jasmine's room, and it reached nearly to the ceiling. Then David fetched the carrying case and placed it on Jasmine's bedroom floor. Jasmine and Tom crouched beside it. The chinchillas were huddled in the corner. They were about the same size as guinea pigs, but they had much larger ears and bushy tails like squirrels' tails, but smaller. Their thick fur was a beautiful silvery-grey colour.

David lifted them out carefully. "This is Daisy," he said, placing one chinchilla in Jasmine's arms, "and this is Clover." He handed her to Tom.

"She's so soft!" exclaimed Jasmine. "I've never felt anything so soft."

"Chinchillas have the softest, densest fur of any animal in the world," said David. "They have up to two hundred thousand hairs per square inch of fur."

"Two hundred *thousand*?" said Tom, looking at Clover's mass of fine hairs. "Per square *inch*?"

"It means they never get fleas, because fleas can't get through the fur to bite them. But it also means they've been hunted nearly to extinction in the wild."

"To make fur coats?" said Jasmine, cuddling Daisy closer to her. "That's so horrible."

"Are they sisters?" asked Tom.

"Yes. Chinchillas are social animals, so it's not good for them to be kept alone. They're much happier with other chinchillas to keep them company."

"Like guinea pigs," said Tom, "and rabbits."

"Can we take them out and play with them?" asked Jasmine.

"Absolutely. Chinchillas need lots of exercise,

so let them out at least once a day. Just make sure you always supervise them, and shut the cage door carefully when you put them back."

Jasmine nodded, stroking Daisy's fur. "I will. I wouldn't want the cats to get anywhere near them."

"There is that," David said, "but actually the cats would find it hard to catch them. They're very agile and fast. They can jump up to six feet, and they're great climbers. The main problem is that they can be incredibly destructive. They gnaw anything they can get their teeth into. I let them run around my living room when I'm in there, but I've had to fix chicken wire to the front of the bookcase since they started chewing the spines off my books."

Jasmine noticed a glass fish bowl on the floor next to the carrying case, filled to about a quarter of the way up with a fine grey powder. "Is that their dust bath?" she asked.

"Yes," said David. "A fish bowl is good because

60

the dust doesn't spill out too much."

Tom looked puzzled. "What's a dust bath?"

"Chinchillas can't wash in water because their fur's too dense, so they have to have a dust bath several times a week," said Jasmine. "I was watching videos online. They roll over and over in this special fine dust and it cleans their fur. It's so fun to watch."

"Well, I'm very grateful to you for looking after them," said David. He took an envelope from his pocket and handed it to Jasmine. "That's a little something for your work."

"Oh, you don't need to pay me," said Jasmine politely.

"No, I insist. Your mum says you're planning to run a boarding kennels alongside your rescue centre when you're older. That sounds like a very sensible business proposition to me. And it must be costing you a fair bit to keep Sky at the moment, so you can put this towards it."

"Well, if you're sure," said Jasmine. "Thank you."

"Just don't leave it lying around," said David, "or Clover and Daisy will have it. I left a twenty-pound note on my bedside table once and they chewed it into a thousand pieces."

Jasmine laughed and stuffed the envelope in her pocket, just as her bedroom door opened and Manu came in.

"Can I see the chinchillas?" he asked. "Oh, they're so cute! Can I hold one?"

"Sure," said David, "if that's OK with Jasmine. She's in charge now."

"Be really careful," said Jasmine, "and support her properly, like this."

"It's your sixth birthday soon, isn't it, Manu?" David said, as Manu stroked Daisy. "What are you hoping to get?"

"A mobility scooter," said Manu.

David looked taken aback. "A what?"

"You know," said Manu. "One of those really cool things old people have, that they ride to the shops on."

"Yes, I know what a mobility scooter is," said David. "I'm just wondering why a six-year-old boy would need one."

"I don't *need* one," explained Manu patiently. "They just look really fun."

"Right," said David. "Of course."

"Do you want one of my cakes?" Manu asked David.

"I wouldn't," said Jasmine, "if I were you."

"Are those the cakes you were making last time I was here?" asked David.

"Yes."

"Oh," said David.

"And you never know," said Manu, "If you're really lucky, you might get the one with the cow's tooth inside it."

Chapter Seven
Completely Ruined

"Open wide," said Jasmine to Sky, prising his jaws apart. "Good boy." She slipped the toothbrush inside his mouth.

It was a week later, and time for Sky's regular grooming session. Jasmine had brushed his coat until it shone, and now she was cleaning his teeth with a soft toothbrush dipped in a weak solution of bicarbonate of soda. Sky stood still, wagging his tail gently from side to side.

"That must taste disgusting," said Tom, who had arrived in the middle of the session. The

65

house was quiet for once. Ella was still at a
friend's house, where she had stayed the previous
night. (Not that Ella ever made any noise
anyway.) Ben had come round earlier, but he had
gone home. Manu was up in his bedroom, Mum
was at work and Dad was out on the farm.

"It tastes revolting," said Jasmine. "I tried it.
But he's very good."

"He adores you so much he'd do anything for
you, that's why," said Tom. And it certainly did
seem that way. Sky never left Jasmine's side if he
could possibly help it.

"Time for your training, Sky," said Jasmine, as
she finished cleaning his teeth.

"I think he's ready for a new challenge with
the finding game," said Tom.

Jasmine clipped Sky's lead to his collar. "What
sort of challenge?"

"Well, he finds you every time now, just by
sniffing you out. Why don't we see if he can find
me?"

"OK," said Jasmine. "Let's try it."

They walked down the garden path. The
weather was dull and overcast this afternoon, the
sky blanketed in thick clouds. The air was still
and sticky, with little black bugs flying around.

"OK, Sky," said Tom, "let's see if you can find
me as well as Jasmine."

The children stood together at the top of
the garden, with Sky sitting beside them. Then
Jasmine unclipped Sky's lead and Tom slowly
began to walk away.

"Find Tom!" commanded Jasmine, sweeping
her left hand away from her in Tom's direction.

Sky looked up at her enquiringly, wagging his
tail. She repeated the command. He followed
her hand movement with his eyes, but he didn't
move.

"Find Tom!" she said again. And, this time,
Sky stood up and, hesitantly at first, trotted off
towards him.

"Good boy!" said Tom, crouching down and

 67

stroking his glossy coat. "Good boy, Sky!"

Jasmine called Sky back and he bounded to
her instantly. "Down!" she said, sweeping her
hand downwards, palm to the ground. Sky
was good at this command now. He lay on the
ground, his eyes fixed on Jasmine, awaiting her
next instruction.

After Sky had run to Tom a few times while
he was in plain view, Tom hid behind a tree
while Sky was watching and Jasmine gave the
command. Sky ran straight to Tom.

"Well done, Sky," said Tom, tickling his tummy
as Sky rolled on his back. "You're a very quick
learner."

"Let's see if he can find you just by your
scent," said Jasmine. "I'll take him round the
corner and you hide."

Just then, a piercing scream came from the
house. Sky shrank back, whining and trembling.
The children stared up at Ella's open bedroom
window, where the scream had come from.

 68

Then they raced towards the back door. Thunder rumbled in the distance as they ran up the stairs.

Ella was sitting on the edge of her bed, her head in her hands, clutching at her hair, rocking backwards and forwards.

"What's happened?" asked Jasmine. "Ella, are you ill? What's wrong?"

Ella sprang off the bed. "That dog of yours, that's what's wrong! Look what he's done to my work! It's completely ruined! All my notes, completely destroyed!"

"By Sky?" said Jasmine. "But how? When?"

With a shaking finger, Ella pointed at the floor behind her. Jasmine and Tom walked round to the other side of her bed. Scattered all over the carpet like confetti were hundreds of minuscule pieces of paper. Paper that, Jasmine could just about make out, had once been Ella's carefully researched, hand-written notes for her summer holiday project.

"That wasn't Sky," said Jasmine. "That was the

chinchillas. Somebody must have left the cage door open."

Ella stared at Jasmine. Her eyes grew huge and her face turned red. Then she strode out to the landing and flung open Manu's bedroom door. Before he could resist, Ella grabbed his arm and dragged him into her room.

"Look at this!" she yelled. "Look at it! Completely ruined! The whole summer holiday I've been working on this and now it's totally destroyed, and all because you are so completely stupid that you can't even shut a cage door!"

"I did shut the door," protested Manu.

"Well, you clearly didn't shut it properly, did you? You complete and utter…"

Ella continued to rant, but Jasmine had stopped listening. She ran into her room, just as the sky darkened and an enormous clap of thunder sounded. The door of the chinchilla cage was open, and there was no sign of Daisy and Clover. Jasmine looked inside their sleeping boxes, but they weren't there either.

She looked up as Tom appeared in the doorway.

"Not there?" he said, and she shook her head. "Where do you think they'll be?"

"Either here or in Ella's room, I guess," said Jasmine.

"Bagsy I search in here," said Tom.

Jasmine took a deep breath and went back to Ella's room.

Ella was still alternately ranting at Manu and sobbing, while fruitlessly scrabbling around picking up tiny pieces of paper. "All that work!

Look at it! And now I'll have to do the whole lot again and I'll never get it finished by the start of term!"

"It's not my fault," Manu was saying. "I definitely shut the door. They must have opened it themselves."

"They can't open it themselves," said Jasmine. "You didn't shut it properly. And you're not even allowed to take them out of the cage when I'm not there, anyway."

Ella started ranting at Manu again. Jasmine turned her back on them and began to search the room. The chinchillas must have been tired after all that chewing. They had probably curled up in a corner somewhere and gone to sleep.

Ella's room wasn't very big and Jasmine searched everywhere. She was going.through all the drawers, looking under Ella's clothes, when Tom reappeared.

"Have you found them?" she asked.

"Yes, and it's so cute. Look at this."

 72

He led the way to Jasmine's room and over
to her bed. Gently, he peeled back the duvet.
And there, in the middle of the bed, snuggled up
together, fast asleep, were two balls of silver-grey
fur.

Jasmine's face broke out in a huge smile. "Oh,
they look so sweet and peaceful. I'm so glad you
found them. I hadn't thought of looking in the
actual bed."

"It's lucky they didn't go to sleep in Ella's bed,"
said Tom, "or Ella would have crushed them."

"It seems a shame to move them," said Jasmine,

"but we'd better put them back."

Tom scooped Daisy into his arms. As Jasmine picked up Clover, an even louder clap of thunder sounded, followed by a dazzling flash.

"Wow, did you see that?" said Tom. "Forked lightning."

Another thunderclap crashed directly overhead, and then came the sound of raindrops drumming on the roof. As they put the chinchillas back in their cage and Jasmine shut the door firmly behind them, her stomach suddenly turned over. In all the panic over Ella and the chinchillas, she hadn't thought about how Sky would react to the storm.

"Where's Sky?" she said.

A worried look came over Tom's face. "Did he follow us upstairs?"

Jasmine ran to the doorway. "Sky!" she called, trying to keep the panic out of her voice. "Sky!"

There was no response.

"Sky!" she called again. "Sky!"

Still nothing.

"I'll search all the rooms upstairs," said Tom. "You do downstairs. He's probably in his bed."

Jasmine ran downstairs, calling Sky's name all the time. She raced into the scullery.

Sky's bed was empty. And the back door was wide open.

Chapter Eight
One of Us
Will Find Him

Jasmine felt sick. She stared through the open
doorway into the pelting rain outside. She had
been the last person to come through that door.
She had left it open. And Sky had gone.

Frantically, she ran through every room
downstairs, looking behind doors and furniture,
under chairs, tables and sofas, any place she could
think of where a traumatised puppy might be
cowering.

Tom appeared as she was making a second
fruitless search of the living room.

"He's not upstairs," he said.

"Did you look under all the beds?"

"I looked under everything, behind everything, in all the cupboards, everywhere. Manu and Ella haven't seen him. Where could he be?"

"I left the back door open," said Jasmine miserably.

Tom's eyes grew wide with horror. "So he's run off."

"He might be miles away by now," said Jasmine. "Dogs just run and run when they're frightened. And he could have gone in any direction. Where do we even start?"

"Why don't you ring your dad? He can go out in his truck around the fields. If Sky's still running, he'll probably spot him. And we can each search in a different direction. One of us will find him."

Grateful for Tom's presence of mind, Jasmine phoned her dad, who was checking the cows, and quickly explained the situation.

"He's going to drive all round the fields," she said to Tom. "And I told him you'll head up to the woods on foot and I'll go down along the river."

They grabbed their coats and tugged on wellies. Jasmine stuffed a handful of Sky's treats in her pocket and gave another handful to Tom. Then they walked out into the pelting rain.

"Don't worry," said Tom. "We'll find him."

Jasmine set off across the farmyard, calling Sky's name, trying not to let panic overwhelm her. A deafening clap of thunder made her jump. Forked lightning lit up the sky ahead.

Suddenly she had a thought so terrible that she almost threw up. What if he had run right

to the edge of the farm and out on to the
main road? What if a car had –

She forced herself to stop imagining such
things. It wouldn't help. She just had to find him.
By the time she had opened the gate to the
sheep field that ran alongside the river, Jasmine
was already soaked, her clothes clinging to
her skin. She walked all around the big field,
calling for Sky, but there was no sign of him.

There was no sign in the next field, either.
With a heavy heart, she climbed over the
gate into the one beyond that. The roar of
car engines and the splashing of tyres were
louder here. The hedge on the far side of this
field bordered the main road.

And then she saw him. Running towards the road, his soaking fur clinging to his body.

"Sky!" she called. "Sky!"

But instead of coming back to her, Sky sped up. Jasmine raced after him, calling his name, but Sky just kept running. When he reached the hedge that bordered the road, he wriggled right into it.

"Stay there!" Jasmine pleaded desperately, as she pelted towards him. "Stay there, Sky!"

She was almost at the hedge when, with one final push, Sky wriggled his way out of the other side and bolted on to the main road, straight into the path of an approaching car.

Jasmine raced to the gate, sick with terror. The car slowed, swerved, and drove on. Jasmine made herself look out into the road. But she saw nothing except cars driving through the rain, headlights on and windscreen wipers at full speed.

And then, in the hedge on the other side of

80

the road, she caught a glimpse of something
white among the thick green leaves.

Was it Sky? She couldn't be sure. To investigate,
she would have to cross the road, something she
was expressly forbidden from doing.

Jasmine looked right and left and right again,
as her parents had drilled into her since she was
a toddler. Only when there was no car visible in
either direction did she cross the road.

She crouched down on the wide verge and
looked into the dense hedgerow. And there, with
his back to her, howling and struggling against
a bramble branch tangled in the fur on his front
legs, was Sky. He was trying to wriggle out of
the other side of the hedge.

Jasmine let out her breath in an enormous sigh of relief.

"Oh, Sky!" she said. "I'm so glad you're safe!"

Sky kept on struggling. Jasmine climbed over the gate into the field and crouched down in front of the hedge on the other side, facing the terrified dog.

"Hello, Sky," she said. "Look, it's me. You're safe now. I've come to get you."

But Sky didn't even seem to recognise her. He just carried on yelping and struggling.

"It's OK, Sky, it's me. Let me get those nasty brambles off you."

Jasmine reached through a gap in the hedge. At that moment, a massive clap of thunder sounded and lightning tore the sky in two. And Sky sank his sharp teeth hard into her hand.

"Ow!" she cried, snatching her hand away.

Tears of shock filled her eyes. She looked at her hand.

There were four bleeding bite marks on it.

Chapter Nine

I Need to Get
You Home

Jasmine sat by the hedge in shock. She couldn't believe what had happened. It had never, ever occurred to her that Sky might bite her.

For some time, she just sat, nursing her sore hand, unable to think straight. Eventually, though, she made herself get her thoughts in order and remember some of the things she had read in her book on collies.

It's because he's frightened, she told herself. That's all it is. He's not an aggressive dog. He hasn't turned wild. He doesn't fear me or hate me. He's just terrified of the storm.

She tried to remember the section in her book about "calming signals" that humans could use to calm stressed or troubled dogs. Canine behaviour experts had learned these signals from watching the body language that dogs use to calm each other in tense situations.

Jasmine got up from the soaking ground and pushed away the hair that was plastered to her face. Sky was still yelping and whimpering in the hedge. Trying to remember the right signals from the book, Jasmine bent over in a play bow, with her arms stretching down in the way a dog would stretch its front legs. Then she sat down again, fairly close to Sky, but with her body turned sideways from him. This would avoid eye contact, which, in his current state, he might see as a threat. She gave a big yawn, to signal that she wasn't being aggressive, and licked the sides of her mouth. Dogs lick their noses, but Jasmine couldn't quite manage that.

Was it just wishful thinking, or were his yelps becoming less frantic?

Jasmine gave another yawn. Then she lowered her face and sniffed the ground. Finally, she stretched out and lay face down on the drenched grass. She was so cold and wet by now that it wouldn't make any difference.

She lay there until Sky had stopped yelping and his cries had quietened to a whimper. She risked a sideways glance at him. He seemed to be trying to reach her. To free him, though, she was going to have to reach into the hedge and disentangle him from the bramble. Would he trust her this time, or would he bite her again?

Slowly, she raised herself to a sitting position, yawning and licking around her mouth to reassure him that she wasn't being aggressive. She remembered the packet of dog treats in her pocket. That might help.

She ripped open the bag with her teeth and put a few treats in her left hand. Her right

 85

hand was too sore to use. Then, still avoiding eye contact, she stretched her arm very slowly through the gap in the hedge.

Holding her breath, desperately hoping there wouldn't be another clap of thunder to spook Sky, Jasmine dropped the dog treats on the ground where he could reach them, and then began to work the bramble out of his coat, yawning and licking the sides of her mouth as she did so.

To her great relief, Sky stretched his neck forward and gobbled up the treats.

"Good boy," said Jasmine softly.

"Good boy, Sky, well done."

She carried on gently disentangling the brambles. He gave a little yelp when she tugged a bit too hard, but apart from that, he was quiet. Finally, Jasmine was able to pull the bramble away, and he was free. She withdrew her hand and sat on the grass again.

Some instinct told her not to call him this time. When she had called him in the field, he had just run away even faster. So she placed the remaining treats in a line from Sky to herself and then sat on the ground, shivering in her saturated clothes, waiting and hoping. The rain slowed to a drizzle, and a glimmer of blue appeared through the clouds.

After a while, she heard Sky move. She glanced sideways and saw that he had stood up. She forced herself to sit still and wait, yawning now to calm herself as much as Sky.

Hesitantly, Sky edged forwards. He was still wearing his lead, but Jasmine resisted the temptation to grab it, in case that panicked him again. She continued to wait.

Sky edged closer and closer, until she could feel the warmth of his breath. And then she felt something that made her heart soar with happiness: Sky's little tongue licking her hand.

"Hello, Sky," she said softly. "Hello, boy. Everything's all right now. Everything's all right."

She wanted to pick him up and cuddle him, but she made herself stay still until she was completely sure he trusted her again. A huge smile spread across her face as he wriggled into her lap, lifted his head and licked her neck.

"Good boy," she said, finally allowing herself to stroke his back. "Good boy, Sky."

Sky snuggled into her lap and licked her face. For a while, she just cuddled him, revelling in the feeling of having him safely back. Then she said, "I need to get you home, Sky. Everyone will be worried about you."

Holding tightly to his lead, Jasmine lifted Sky gently off her lap. Then, stiff from the cold and from sitting motionless on the hard wet ground, she got to her feet and set off for home.

Chapter Ten
What Happened to Your Hand?

When Jasmine got home, the house was empty. She phoned her dad, who was very relieved to hear the news. It turned out that not only Tom, but Manu, and even Ella, were out looking for Sky.

"I'll round up the others in the truck," Dad said, "and we'll be back as soon as we can."

Jasmine took the shivering dog out to the scullery and wrapped him in an old towel. She gave him food and water, rubbed him dry and brushed his coat. When the key turned in the front door, she assumed it was Dad with the others, so she was surprised when her mother walked into the scullery.

"Oh, Jasmine," she said, "you're absolutely drenched. Are you all right?"

"I'm fine," said Jasmine. "It was Sky who wasn't."

"I just got Dad's messages," said Mum. "I was in surgery. Any injuries?"

"No, thank goodness," said Jasmine, as she finished brushing his coat. "He was caught in brambles, but only his fur. He walked home with me and I think he's fine, except he must be really tired."

"To your bed, Sky," said Mum, pointing to Sky's crate. He walked in and curled straight up in his bed.

"He should sleep well," said Mum. "It's you I'm worried about. You look absolutely frozen. Take those wet clothes off and let's get you in the bath."

After her bath, Jasmine went down to the kitchen in her pyjamas and dressing gown. Mum made hot chocolate and toasted teacakes.

"Dad's just taking Tom home," she said, "and then he'll be back with the others."

She slid a mug of hot chocolate across the table. Jasmine stretched out her hand to take it. Mum frowned.

"What's happened to your hand?"

Jasmine pulled it back. "Oh, I just caught it on

the brambles."

"Let me see."

"It's fine, honestly."

"Jasmine, show me your hand," said Mum, in her sternest voice.

With a twisting knot in her stomach, Jasmine held her hand out.

Mum looked at her in horror. "Sky *bit* you?"

Tears filled Jasmine's eyes. She tried to blink them back. "He didn't mean to. He was frightened of the thunder. It was all my fault."

Every muscle in her body was tense, waiting for Mum to say, "I warned you this might happen. It's not safe. We can't keep him here any longer."

But instead, Mum said gently, "Tell me all about it."

So, while Mum cleaned the bite wounds, Jasmine told her everything. The only thing she left out was the fact that Sky, and therefore she, had crossed the main road. This part, she felt, was not essential to the story and would only cause unnecessary fuss.

When she had finished, she waited with bated breath for Mum's verdict. Mum was silent for a nerve-wrackingly long time. Finally, she said, "Well, the good news is, once he had bitten you, you did all the right things. It was lucky you'd read about calming signals. It sounds as though you used them very effectively."

She paused. Jasmine stayed tense and expectant. Mum clearly had more to say.

"Your mistakes were all in the build-up to the bite," said Mum. "Sky didn't want to hurt you. He loves you more than anything. But at that point, he was simply acting from his deepest instincts. Your big mistake, apart from leaving the door open in the first place, was to call him back when you went looking for him."

Jasmine stared at her. "What do you mean? How else would he come back?"

"I know it goes against all your instincts," said

 94

Mum, "but the one thing you really shouldn't do with a dog that's run off in fear, is call it. The noise that spooked him brought out his fight or flight response, you see, and a dog's instinct in that situation is just to run and run, to get as far away as possible from the perceived danger. If you call him back, he just keeps on running, because his instincts tell him not to allow himself to be caught."

"So what should I have done?" asked Jasmine.

"Well, when you saw him," said Mum, "you should have kept a bit of distance and used the calming signals, so that, eventually, he would calm down and come to you. When you put your hand in the hedge to try to catch him, he was so panicked that he probably didn't even recognise you. He just saw you as another threat. And it was particularly unfortunate that there happened to be a thunderclap at that moment. Dogs have such sensitive hearing that thunder must sound absolutely terrifying to them."

"You're not going to send him away because he bit me, are you?" said Jasmine. "You know he didn't mean to. And he won't do it again. I'm sure he won't."

"There's no point even discussing it at the moment," said Mum. "It's not quite been a month since we reported him to the dog warden. Somebody still might come forward and claim him."

"Nobody's going to claim him," said Jasmine. "They left him in a hedge to die. You're just saying that because you don't want to talk about it."

"You're right," said Mum. "I don't want to talk about it. I just want to make dinner in peace."

Jasmine went to her room, tired but very relieved. Mum hadn't said she would send Sky away, and Jasmine was sure that nobody would claim him now. There were only four days left until the month was up. And then Sky would be hers forever.

 96

Chapter Eleven

She Can't Take Sky Away

Three days later, Jasmine, Tom and Sky were playing hide and seek. Jasmine held Sky on his lead around the corner of the house, where Mum was weeding the flowerbed, while Tom went to hide in the orchard. Sky was getting to be a very good seeker, so they were hiding further and further away.

Jasmine gave Tom a couple of minutes to hide, and then she unclipped Sky's lead and said, "Find Tom!"

Sky trotted off happily, his nose to the ground

and his tail wagging.
Jasmine followed at a
distance. Tom was crouched
behind a patch of nettles in the
far corner of the orchard, and Sky
found him easily. While Tom was
praising him, Jasmine petted Truffle,
who was digging up the grass under
an apple tree with her tough snout.
The huge sow grunted contentedly as
Jasmine scratched her behind the ears.

"It will soon be autumn, Truffle," said

Jasmine, looking up at the enormous old oak
tree in the corner of the orchard, "and you'll
have all those acorns to feast on."

"Do you want to hide," said Tom, "or shall I go
again?"

"You hide one more time," said Jasmine, "and
then let's go to the den."

Yesterday, she and Tom had started building
a den in the thicket at the bottom of the horse
paddock. (There were no horses in the horse
paddock now, but the field had got its name in
the days before tractors were invented, when the
farm horses used to graze there.)

Jasmine gave Truffle a final scratch behind the
ears and then called Sky. He started to run in
front of her as they headed for the gate, and she
gave the command she had learned from Tom's
Aunty Angela. "Stay close!"

Sky turned and came back to her immediately.
"Good boy," she said. "Good boy, Sky."

At the orchard gate, she made sure Sky stayed

 99

behind her so that she could go through the gate first. Angela had told her that this was really important.

"Always remember that dogs are pack animals," Angela had said. "They're always looking to move up the pecking order. When they try to push past you in gateways, it's because they're trying to be top dog. It's really important that you don't let them get away with it. You must always be top dog. And Sky will want to please you, so if you're consistent, he'll quickly learn what he needs to do to earn your praise."

Sky certainly wanted to please Jasmine, and he was also a quick learner. Jasmine had read that border collies are the most intelligent dogs in the world, and Sky, she was sure, was one of the most intelligent border collies of them all. She couldn't wait until he was a few months older and she could start training him to work sheep.

Mum's phone started to ring as Jasmine came around the corner. Her mother pulled off

 100

her gardening gloves and fished it out of her back pocket. She glanced at the screen before answering.

"Hello, Linda, what's up?"

Linda was the head nurse at Mum's surgery. Mum listened for a minute, and then said, "Are you sure she means Sky?"

Linda said something else. "Uh-huh," said Mum, nodding and listening intently. Linda spoke for what felt like ages. Mum shot a glance at Jasmine, who was standing rigid, staring at her.

"Yes, yes, I'll come in," Mum said, standing up and brushing the debris off her jeans. "Give her a cup of tea and tell her I'll be there in twenty minutes."

"What was that?" asked Jasmine, as Mum ended the call. "What was Linda saying about Sky?"

Mum took a deep breath.

"A woman has just come into the surgery. She says she's the sister of Sky's owner."

Jasmine stared at her in horror. "No. It can't be Sky. It could be any collie. Why does she think it's Sky?"

"She's brought in photos of a puppy that she says belonged to her brother. And Linda says the dog has exactly the same markings as Sky."

"No," said Jasmine. "It's not Sky. Lots of collies have those markings. She's got no proof."

"Well, that's why I'm going in now. To have a look at these photos and get more details from her."

"I'm coming too," said Jasmine. "She can't have him. She can't take Sky away."

Mum walked over to her and put her hands on Jasmine's shoulders.

"I'm sorry, Jas, but I can't take you with me."

"But I have to come!"

Mum shook her head. "This could be a tricky situation and it has to be handled professionally. I need to go on my own."

"But I have to be there. Sky is my dog!"

Mum opened her mouth as though she was about to say something, and then closed it again. Jasmine stared at her. She knew what Mum had been about to say. Sky wasn't her dog. Sky had another owner, and that owner was about to claim him back.

"Jasmine, what are you doing?" called Tom, walking towards her. "I've been waiting ages."

Jasmine turned her back on her mother. "Let's go to the den," she said to Tom. "And afterwards, let's go to your house. I'm not coming back here again."

Chapter Twelve
It Doesn't Make Sense

Jasmine was almost speechless with anger as she and Tom walked across the horse paddock with Sky.

"How could she?" she said. "She's a traitor, going to see this woman. And she wouldn't even let me go with her. I've got a right to go. I'm the one who's been looking after Sky all this time."

"Why would an owner wait nearly a month after their dog had disappeared before they looked for it?" said Tom. "It doesn't make sense. I bet her brother isn't really the owner. I bet she just wants to get a dog for free and she's gone round all the vets asking if they've had any stray collies brought in, until she found one that had."

Jasmine gazed at him, open-mouthed. "Yes!" she said. "Of course! And that's why she's pretending to be the owner's sister, not the owner. Because then it won't look so suspicious if she can't answer all the questions."

"But even if her brother is Sky's owner," said Tom, "they won't give Sky back to him, will they? He left him in a hedge to die."

"Exactly," said Jasmine. But then a thought struck her. A thought so terrible that she stopped dead in her tracks. Sky pulled on the lead, trying to keep on walking, and Jasmine automatically gave the command, "Stay close!" Sky turned and looked at her enquiringly, and then moved back to stand beside her.

"What?" asked Tom. "What's wrong?"

"What if his owner didn't leave him to die?" said Jasmine. "What if there was a storm, or fireworks, or something else that spooked him, and he ran off and got caught in the hedge and couldn't get free, exactly like the other day? What if his owner really loved him and he's been searching for him ever since?" A huge lump rose in her throat so that she could hardly speak. "I thought he was my dog, but what if he's not? What if he had another owner who loved him and has been missing him all this time?"

The lump in her throat was so big by now that she couldn't speak any more. She quickened her pace, Sky trotting beside her. Tom walked beside her too, and he didn't say anything. *That's because he knows I'm right*, thought Jasmine, *and there's nothing he can say to make me feel better. Sky is going to be taken away from me, and there's nothing anyone can do about it.*

At the end of the field, they climbed over the gate and Tom headed towards their den.

"Do you mind if we don't go to the den?" said Jasmine. "I don't really feel like it today. Can we

 106

just keep walking?"

"Sure," said Tom, and they carried on towards the woods.

After a minute, Tom said, "I don't think that's right."

"What's not right?"

"What you said about Sky running off from his last owner and getting stuck in that hedge."

"Why don't you think it's right?"

"Well, Sky wasn't stuck when you found him, was he?"

"No," said Jasmine. "But he could have wriggled free eventually, and then been too weak by that time to get out of the hedge."

Tom pushed out his bottom lip thoughtfully. "Maybe," he said. "Did it look like he'd been there a long time? Was the ground all bare around him? Did it look like a dog had been frantically trying to get free for ages?"

Jasmine pictured the scene in her mind's eye. The tiny little puppy in the hedge, whimpering for help.

"No," she said. "I don't think so. I don't remember the ground being bare. And also," she said, her eyes growing large as she looked at Tom, "it would have been really smelly if he'd been there for ages, wouldn't it? If he'd been using it as a toilet all that time?"

"Really smelly," agreed Tom.

"And it wasn't. I mean, it was a *bit* smelly – *he* was a bit smelly, poor thing – but not like he'd been there for long enough to turn a healthy dog into a starving one."

"And also," said Tom, "if he'd been there all that time, I bet someone would have found him earlier. I mean, you heard him whining, didn't you? And he was quite near the track."

"And that track's a public footpath," said Jasmine. "Lots of people use it. Dog walkers. I bet another dog would have found him and alerted their owner."

"Exactly," said Tom. "So I don't believe he got

stuck there. I think he was already
starving, and someone just left him there
to die."

"But how can we prove that?" asked
Jasmine. "What if these people are really
good liars, and Mum believes them?"

"They must need to have proof," said Tom.
"And why would anybody want a dog back
if they'd thrown it out in the first place?
I don't get it. Maybe," he said, turning to
Jasmine, "maybe this woman wants to
report her brother for cruelty, and that's
why she's got in touch."

"Maybe," said Jasmine doubtfully. "But
then why didn't she just phone the
RSPCA?"

Tom shrugged. "I don't know."

They walked around the woods for
a while, but it wasn't a happy walk.
Sky seemed to be able to sense
that something wasn't right

with Jasmine, and he stayed very close, glancing at her frequently.

After a while, Tom's phone beeped in his pocket. He looked at the message.

"I have to go home for tea," he said. "Are you coming?"

Jasmine thought for a moment. Then she said, "No, I'm going to carry on walking for a bit. I'll go home later. But thanks anyway."

Privately, she had no intention of going home for many hours yet. She hoped her mum would get very worried about her. It would serve her right.

Chapter Thirteen
Might It Be Possible?

Once Tom had gone and Jasmine had no one to distract her, it was impossible to stop the terrible thoughts from flooding into her head. What if Sky really had just run off and got stuck in that hedge? What if the owner or his sister was right now showing Mum all the photos they had taken of Sky as a much-loved puppy, photos that proved Sky was really theirs?

Or, even worse – so terrible that it gave Jasmine physical pain to think about it – what if Sky's owner had been cruel to him and starved him, but now, for some reason, he wanted him back? What if he had proof that Sky was his, and convinced Mum that he was a kind owner, but then when he got him back he planned to shut him up and starve him again?

Jasmine climbed the gate that led out of the woods into a field on the other side. She walked across the field, faster and faster, Sky trotting to keep up with her. She was blinded by tears and by the terrible visions in her head. She didn't know where she was going; she only knew she had to keep walking. As long as she and Sky were together, away from anyone who would try to separate them, that was all that mattered.

Suddenly her left foot, instead of landing on solid ground, sank deep into a rabbit hole. Jasmine lost her balance and crashed down, twisting her trapped ankle and falling with a thud on to the hard ground.

The pain in her ankle was so extreme that, for some time, she just lay on the ground, crying out

 112

and moaning. Then she felt Sky licking her nose.
Still moaning in pain, she lifted her arm to stroke
him. Gingerly, she heaved herself up to a sitting
position so she could inspect the damage.

She was shocked to see that her ankle was
already swollen. Was it broken? If she had broken
it, how could she care for Sky?

The ankle hurt even more when she touched it. The swelling was hurting her foot, so, very carefully, she unlaced her trainer and took it off, wincing as every movement sent fresh pain shooting through her body. She had no strength left to take off her sock. She just sat on the ground, moaning in pain, with Sky licking her face and hands, trying, she was sure, to make her feel better.

"You're such a good dog," she said. "And you do make me feel better. You really do."

Slowly and carefully, she shifted all her weight on to her right side and, using her hands to push herself upright, tried to stand. When she put even the smallest amount of weight on her swollen ankle, it hurt so much she almost threw up. Eventually she managed to get herself into a standing position, but as soon as she tried to put any weight on her injured ankle, the pain was unbearable. How was she going to get home?

If she had still been in the wood, she might

have been within reach of a makeshift crutch, but here, there wasn't a stick in sight. She was well and truly stranded. And she couldn't stand on one leg for much longer.

Placing her hands on the ground, she carefully lowered herself back to a sitting position.

How long would it be before they came looking for her?

She had told her mum she was going to Tom's. Nobody would be expecting her at home for hours. And she had told Tom she was going home, so he wouldn't be expecting her at all. Even when they did start searching, it might be hours before they found her. And rainclouds were gathering in the sky.

Sky licked her face. And suddenly Jasmine had a thought.

What if…?

Might it be possible? Might Sky be able to find Tom?

It would be much more of a challenge than

any game of hide and seek they had played before. Sky would have to go back to the wood before he would even pick up Tom's scent.

Would he do this on his own? And if he did get to the wood, he would have to trace the scent all the way through the wood and across a big field to Tom's house. Luckily, there were no roads to cross, but still, it was a long way for Sky. And if he reached Tom's house, how would he let Tom know he was there? Jasmine couldn't bear to think of Sky sitting patiently outside the house for hours, alone and unnoticed.

Sky gave a little bark and made an impatient movement.

"You want me to get up and walk, don't you?" said Jasmine. "But I can't walk."

Sky circled her, nose to the ground, tail wagging. He looked as though he had plenty of energy.

"Would you like to do a job for me, Sky?"
Sky licked her face again.

 116

Jasmine made up her mind.

"Lie down," she commanded.

Sky didn't even need the hand signal any more. He lay on the ground, fully alert, his tail sweeping across the grass from side to side, his eyes completely focused on Jasmine's face, awaiting his next instruction.

"Find Tom," said Jasmine, sweeping her hand away towards the woods. "Find Tom!"

Sky sprang to his feet. He trotted off towards the woods, sniffing at the ground. Then he turned to look back at Jasmine.

"Find Tom!" she called, sweeping her hand
away again. "Find Tom!"

Sky put his nose back to the ground and
continued across the field. At the gate that
led into the woods, where Jasmine and Tom
had parted, he started to wag his tail and sniff
excitedly at the grass.

"You've found Tom's scent," said Jasmine.
"Good dog, Sky."

She said this very quietly, so as not to distract
him from his task. She didn't want him to think
he'd completed the job already.

Sky slipped under the gate and trotted off into
the woods. Jasmine watched him until she could

no longer see him through the trees.

Once he was out of sight, she felt acutely alone. Without Sky to focus on, the throbbing pain in her ankle was much harder to bear. She lay on the ground and looked up at the heavy grey clouds amassing above her. There was nothing more she could do. Exhaustion overwhelmed her and she closed her eyes.

Jasmine woke up, stiff and aching, on the cold, hard ground. It was getting dark. Her ankle throbbed. Slowly and painstakingly, she manoeuvred herself into a sitting position. A vast purple bruise now covered her swollen ankle. How long had she been asleep?

Was that voices in the distance, or was she imagining it?

She heard light footsteps running through the grass, and the panting of a dog. She turned to see Sky bounding across the field towards her, barking joyfully. Behind him, at the edge of the woods, was Tom.

Chapter Fourteen
What's Going to Happen to Sky?

While they were waiting for Dad to arrive in the truck, Tom told Jasmine what had happened. He had been up in his bedroom when he'd heard a scrabbling and whining at the front door. He had opened the door to find Sky on the step.

"At first," he said, "I thought you'd changed your mind and decided to come to my house after all. I called you, but you didn't come, so I thought you must have sent Sky ahead to find me. So I told him to find you, and he just kept going back through the woods. I couldn't believe you'd have sent him all that way, so I kept stopping and calling you. But Sky never stopped. He just kept on going, and he led me right here. He was amazing."

"He's an amazing dog," said Jasmine. "Aren't you, Sky?"

Dad took Jasmine to the hospital, where she was very relieved to discover that she had no broken bones, just a nasty sprain. She was told to get plenty of rest and treat her ankle with ice for three days. She wasn't to put weight on it for a week. And she was given crutches, which made the situation seem a lot more fun.

"I think we'd better get you a phone of your own," said Dad, as they drove home. Seeing the look of delight on Jasmine's face, he hastily said, "Nothing fancy, just a basic one, so you can call us if you get into any more sticky situations."

As they drove down the farm track, Jasmine saw Mum's car in the farmyard. She felt sick again. What had happened at the surgery? Was Sky about to be taken away from her?

When Jasmine walked into the house on her crutches, Manu's mouth fell open.

"You've got crutches? That is so cool. Can I have a go? Give them to me."

Mum came running downstairs and enfolded Jasmine in a tight hug. "Oh, my goodness, Jasmine, what are we going to do with you? Come into the living room and put your feet up, and I'll get some ice for your poor ankle."

"Dad's getting the ice," said Jasmine. "What did the woman say? Does Sky really belong to her brother? What's going to happen?"

But Mum wouldn't tell her anything until she was lying on the sofa with her left foot raised on a pillow, ice packs on her ankle and Sky on the floor beside her. Jasmine gave Manu her crutches to play on, provided he played in another room. Ella sat at the dining table, hunched over Mum's laptop, books spread out all around her. Mum had suggested that she did her notes on a computer this time, to make them more chinchilla-proof. Ella had clearly forgiven the chinchillas, though, as they were both snuggled up in her lap.

"They're just so soft," she said, when Jasmine expressed her surprise. "They're very comforting animals. When they're asleep, anyway."

"You must be starving, Jas," said Mum.

"What would you like? Pasta? Beans on toast?"

"I'm not hungry," said Jasmine. "Just tell me about Sky."

Manu's head appeared round the doorframe. "These are the best things ever," he said. "When your ankle's better, can I keep them?"

"Sure," said Jasmine. "Mum, tell me about Sky. *Please*."

Mum sat in the armchair opposite Jasmine. "Well," she said, "the woman who came into the surgery – Iris, she's called – *is* the sister of Sky's former owner. She brought in photos of him at two months old, and the dates she gave, of his age and of his disappearance, matched up with our dates."

Jasmine couldn't speak. It really was going to happen. Sky was going to be taken away from her.

"Her brother bought Sky on a whim, it seems," said Mum, "as an eight-week-old puppy. Iris said he made a fuss of Sky at first – his name wasn't Sky then, of course – but the next time she visited, two months later, Sky was tied up in a shed, and looked skinny and uncared-for.

 126

She lives sixty miles away, so she doesn't see her brother very often."

"So why didn't she report him then?" asked Jasmine, furiously.

"Her brother told her that the dog had been ill with worms, and that was why he was thin and sick-looking. He said he was treating him."

"And she believed him?"

"It sounds as though this man is a nasty piece of work, and I got the feeling that Iris was afraid to get on the wrong side of him. She said she phoned a few times, and he told her Sky was better. But when she came to visit today, there was no sign of him, and her brother told her he'd died. She was suspicious, and she asked which vet had been treating him. He gave her the name of my practice, so she came in on her way home to check his story. Of course, her brother had never been there, but when Iris told Linda about it and showed her the photos, Linda realised that the dog must be Sky."

 127

"Why would he get a dog," Jasmine said, "if he didn't even want to look after it?"

"Sadly," said Mum, "all too many people do. They fall in love with a cute puppy, but have no idea of the hours they're going to have to spend training and looking after it, every single day for the next fifteen years. Collies suffer more than most. They're incredibly cute puppies, but they've been bred over centuries to be working dogs, not pets. They grow into extremely energetic dogs, who need very careful training and masses of exercise. People can't cope with them, and then they blame the dog for being too demanding or badly behaved. Rehoming centres are full of collies whose owners just didn't bother to consider what they were taking on."

The back door opened and Jasmine heard Dad taking his boots off in the scullery.

"We phoned the RSPCA, and an inspector is going to his house," said Mum. "He'll be prosecuted, and probably banned from keeping an animal again."

"He'd better be," said Jasmine. "He should be put in prison for life."

"He should be starved and thrown in a hedge to die," said Manu, hopping into the room on Jasmine's crutches. "I'm starving, Mum. What can I have to eat?"

"There might be some biscuits left," said Mum. "But don't eat too many. Dad's going to make dinner in a minute."

Manu hopped out of the room.

"Careful," said Dad, coming into the hall. "We don't want any more sprained ankles today."

"But what's going to happen to Sky?" asked Jasmine.

Mum and Dad looked at each other.

"We've been thinking about this," said Dad.

 129

"I could really do with a sheepdog if I'm going to increase the flock. And Sky certainly seems to have the makings of a good working dog. So we wondered if you'd be prepared, Jasmine, to work with me to train Sky as a sheepdog."

Jasmine stared from her mum to her dad, hardly able to take this in.

"You mean … I can really keep him?"

"You've done very well with his training so far," said Dad, "and he's clearly keen and quick. So if you're happy to share him with me, then yes, we think it would be a good idea to keep him."

"Oh, thank you!" cried Jasmine, flinging her arms around Sky's neck. "Sky, did you hear that?"

"Yay!" cried Manu, running into the room. They all looked at him curiously.

"I didn't realise you were so keen to keep Sky," said Mum.

"Of course I am," said Manu, "but it's not that." He brandished a half-eaten cupcake in the air. "Look! There was one left in the tin, and it had the lucky tooth inside it!"

"Excellent," said Dad. "And I'm sure we're all very happy that you were the one who found it."

Jasmine turned back to Sky. "First I rescued you," she said, "and then you rescued me. And now you're going to stay here forever. And, even better than that, Sky, you're going to do what collies love to do more than anything else in the world. You're going to be a sheepdog."

Look out for more
of Jasmine's adventures!

Coming soon!

Look out for more amazing animal adventures at the Rescue Zoo!